Grandma Lena's
Big Ol' Turnip

Denia Lewis Hester

Illustrated by

Jackie Urbanovic

To Mark Lewis, Michelle McDonald, and
Jennifer and Chris Williams—D.L.H.

For Annie and her family: Devon, Andela, Philip, Olivia,
Jay, Shanelle, Kayla, Keria, Kaya, and Najay.
The hours they spent pulling up an
imaginary turnip made these
paintings possible—J.U.

Library of Congress Cataloging-in-Publication Data

Hester, Denia Lewis.
Grandma Lena's big ol' turnip / written by Denia Lewis Hester ; illustrated
by Jackie Urbanovic.
p. cm.
Summary: Grandma Lena grows a turnip so big that it takes her entire family to
pull it up, and half of the town to eat it. Includes a note about cooking "soul food."
ISBN 0-8075-3027-1 (hardcover)
[1. Turnips–Fiction. 2. Cookery, American–Southern style–Fiction. 3. African Americans—Fiction.
4. Tall tales.] I. Title: Grandma Lena's big ol' turnip. II. Urbanovic, Jackie, ill. III. Title.
PZ7.H4377Gr 2005 [E]—dc22 2004018580

Text copyright © 2005 by Denia Lewis Hester. Illustrations copyright © 2005 by Jackie Urbanovic.
Published in 2005 by Albert Whitman & Company, 6340 Oakton Street, Morton Grove, Illinois 60053-2723.
Published simultaneously in Canada by Fitzhenry & Whiteside, Markham, Ontario.
All rights reserved. No part of this book may be reproduced or transmitted in any form or by any means,
electronic or mechanical, including photocopying, recording, or by any information storage and
retrieval system, without permission in writing from the publisher.
Printed in China through Colorcraft, Ltd., Hong Kong.
10 9 8 7 6 5 4 3 2 1

The design is by Carol Gildar.

For more information about Albert Whitman & Company,
please visit our web site at www.albertwhitman.com.

A note about the story

Grandma Lena's Big Ol' Turnip was adapted from a Russian folk tale, "The Turnip," as told by Aleksey Tolstoy. This popular cumulative tale appeared in the mid-1800s in a collection by Russian historian and folklorist Aleksandr Nikolayevich Afanas'ev (1826–1871).

The meal Grandma serves is an example of traditional African-American cookery. Turnip, mustard, or collard greens are usually boiled with a small piece of ham, bacon, or pork fat to season them. Corn bread baked in the oven or fried in a cast iron skillet is often served with the greens. (Grandma Lena made corn muffins.) The meal might include a pot of beans, like Great Northern, or black-eyed peas. This kind of cooking is often called "soul food" or just Southern-style cooking.

White Knight

The whole thing started when Grandma Lena decided to grow turnips in her backyard garden.

With her reading glasses perched on her nose, all winter she studied her seed catalogs, hoping to find just the right kind to plant. Grandma chuckled at all the fancy names. There were White Knights and Scarlet Queens. Royal Crown and White Lady. She finally decided on a turnip called Purple Top. After all, purple was her favorite color.

Purple Top

When spring arrived and the ground was soft enough for digging, Grandma Lena planted the tiny seeds. She didn't worry that the air was still nippy. She knew turnips liked cool weather.

Soon, tiny plants popped up.

For the next month, Grandma Lena watered and weeded her turnip plants every day.

"Hey, Lena," Uncle Isadore teased. "I hope you taught those turnips how to swim. You're watering them so much I'm afraid they're gonna drown!"

Grandma Lena grunted and said what she always believed. "Anything worth doing is worth doing right."

Every day the turnips grew.
One was bigger than the rest.

On the first day of June, Grandma Lena stepped into her garden to find the biggest, fattest, most gigantic turnip she had ever laid eyes on. "What a fine turnip stew it will make!" she thought. "It's enough to feed half the town!"

From the porch, Baby Pearl stared at the turnip with wide eyes. "Big potato!" she said with a giggle.

Grandma Lena took hold of the enormous stem and leaves. She yanked and jerked and tugged, but that big ol' turnip would not budge.

"Carl!" Grandma called. "Put down that newspaper and help me pull up this big ol' turnip."

Grandpa took off his reading glasses and came running. Then Grandpa pulled on Grandma while Grandma pulled at the turnip. They yanked and jerked and tugged, but that big ol' turnip would not budge.

"Iz-zy!" Grandma yelled. "Stop eating up my peach jam and help us pull up this big ol' turnip!"

Uncle Isadore wiped his mouth and came running. Uncle Isadore pulled on Grandpa, Grandpa pulled on Grandma, and they yanked and jerked and tugged, but that big ol' turnip would not budge.

"Netty!" Grandma yelled. "Put the baby down and help us pull up this big ol' turnip!"

Aunt Netty gave Baby Pearl a toy and came running. Aunt Netty pulled on Uncle Isadore, Uncle Isadore pulled on Grandpa, and Grandpa pulled on Grandma. They yanked and jerked and tugged, but that big ol' turnip would not budge.

"Rascal!" Grandma hollered. "Put down that bone and help us pull up this big ol' turnip!"

Rascal dropped his chew bone and came running. Then Rascal pulled on Aunt Netty, Aunt Netty pulled on Uncle Isadore, Uncle Isadore pulled on Grandpa, and Grandpa pulled on Grandma.

They yanked and jerked and tugged, but that big ol' turnip *would not budge!*

Baby Pearl came toddling across the yard, her diaper half undone.

"Shame on us," said Grandma. "We forgot about Pearl."

Baby Pearl pointed at the ground. "Big potato!" she said.

"Stand back, Pearl," warned Grandma. "I'm going to haul this turnip out if it's the last thing I do! Okay, everyone, PULL!"

In all the confusion nobody noticed that Baby Pearl was holding onto Rascal's tail. Then Rascal clamped onto Cousin Netty's skirt, Cousin Netty grabbed Uncle Isadore, Uncle Isadore grabbed Grandpa, and Grandpa held tight to Grandma.

The whole family yanked and jerked and tugged with all their strength.

POP!

At last, with dirt flying in all directions, that big ol' turnip burst out of the ground— and the whole family fell in a pile behind it!

Baby Pearl clapped and said, "Uh-oh! Faw down!"

By now the sun was setting. Everyone else went to bed, exhausted, but Grandma Lena stayed up late. She washed and chopped the turnip greens and put them in her biggest pots with some onions and bacon and cooked them until they were nice and tender.

After that she chopped up the giant turnip. It was so big there would be plenty left over for turnip casseroles, turnip fries, and pickled turnips.

Then she made a turnip stew with potatoes, carrots, and peas.

What would turnip stew be without corn bread? thought Lena. So she baked golden brown corn muffins.

The next day, Grandma Lena invited all her friends and neighbors to help her fill in the hole and share her delicious turnip dishes. Half the town showed up with shovels, hoes, and spades. Some brought jugs of cool apple cider and lemony tea cakes to share.

It was the biggest party since last year's Fourth-of-July picnic. Everyone agreed that it was the best meal they'd had in a long, long time.

The neighbors joked about what Grandma Lena would plant next year. "It'll be big," one neighbor said. "Lena doesn't do anything halfway!"

"Of course," said Grandma Lena.
"Anything worth doing is worth doing right."

That night, when the family was full and dozing in their chairs,
Baby Pearl whispered to Rascal, "Big potato aw gone!"